THREE
TWO
ONE
DAY

THREE
TWO
ONE
DAY

Written by Debbie Driscoll · Illustrated by Lynne Woodcock Cravath

Simon & Schuster Books for Young Readers
Published by Simon & Schuster
New York • London • Toronto • Sydney • Tokyo • Singapore

SIMON & SCHUSTER BOOKS FOR YOUNG READERS
Simon & Schuster Building, Rockefeller Center, 1230 Avenue of the Americas,
New York, New York 10020. Text copyright © 1994 by Debbie Driscoll. Illustrations
copyright © 1994 by Lynne Cravath. All rights reserved including the right of
reproduction in whole or in part in any form. SIMON & SCHUSTER BOOKS FOR
YOUNG READERS is a trademark of Simon & Schuster.

Designed by David Neuhaus.
The text of this book is set in 22 pt. Baskerville.
The illustrations were done in pen and ink and watercolor.
Manufactured in the United States of America   10 9 8 7 6 5 4 3 2 1

Library of Congress Cataloging-in-Publication Data
Driscoll, Debbie. Three two one day / by Debbie Driscoll ; illustrated
by Lynne Cravath. Summary: Illustrations and rhyming text describe the
activities enjoyed on each day of the week.
[1. Days—Fiction.   2. Stories in rhyme.]
I. Cravath, Lynne, ill.   II. Title.
PZ8.3.D8324Th 1994 [E]—dc20 CIP 92-23420
ISBN 0-671-79330-6

For Ardi Arrington…she knows why—DD

For Jay, Chloe and Jeff, with love—LWC

Wake on Monday.

Where's the sun day?

Chores get done day,
then some fun day.

Bake on Monday,
cinnamon bun day.

Tales are spun day,
story time Monday.

Bike on Tuesday,
win or lose day.

Crash and bruise day,
black-and-blue day.

Hike on Tuesday,
muddy shoes day.

Squishy ooze day,
explore on Tuesday.

Draw on Wednesday,
crayons and pens day.

Count to ten day,

sort and spend day.

Sing on Wednesday,
see my friends day.

Stretch and bend day,
class on Wednesday.

Dig on Thursday,
trucks grind *grrr* day.

Clank and whir day,
pour and stir day.

Bath on Thursday,
scrub off dirt day.

Squeeze and squirt day,
clean on Thursday.

Shop on Friday,
find and buy day.

Pile cart high day,

boxes fly day.

Snack on Friday,
milk and pie day.

Mom's and my day,
together on Friday.

Paint on Saturday,
climb the ladder day.

Clothes all tattered day,
splash and splatter day.

Stop on Saturday.

What's the matter day?

Pitter-patter day,
rain on Saturday.

Visit on Sunday,
chase and run day.

Games are won day,
silly fun day.

Hide on Sunday,
three two one day.

Ice-cream sundae,
week is done day.